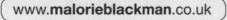

# FANGS

www.**malorieblackman**.co.uk

# FANGS

# Malorie
# Blackman

## Illustrated by Jamie Smith

Tamarind

FANGS

A TAMARIND BOOK 978 1 848 53142 0

First published in Great Britain in 1998 by Orchard Books

This edition published by Tamarind,
an imprint of Random House Children's Publishers UK
A Penguin Random House Company

Penguin
Random House
UK

This edition published 2015

1 3 5 7 9 10 8 6 4 2

Penguin Random House is committed to a sustainable future for our
business, our readers and our planet. This book is made from
Forest Stewardship Council® certified paper.

MIX
Paper from
responsible sources
FSC® C018179

Set in Bembo MT Schoolbook 16/21pt

Tamarind Books are published by Random House Children's Publishers UK,
61–63 Uxbridge Road, London W5 5SA

www.**randomhousechildrens**.co.uk
www.**totallyrandombooks**.co.uk
www.**randomhouse**.co.uk

Addresses for companies within The Random House Group Limited can be found
at: www.randomhouse.co.uk/offices.htm

THE RANDOM HOUSE GROUP Limited Reg. No. 954009

A CIP catalogue record for this book is available from the British Library.

Printed and bound by CPI Group (UK) Ltd, Croydon, CR0 4YY

*For Neil and Lizzy,*
*with love as always.*

**Malorie Blackman** has written over sixty books and is acknowledged as one of today's most imaginative and convincing writers for young readers. She has been awarded numerous prizes for her work, including the Red House Children's Book Award and the Fantastic Fiction Award. Malorie has also been shortlisted for the Carnegie Medal. In 2005 she was honoured with the Eleanor Farjeon Award in recognition of her contribution to children's books, and in 2008 she received an OBE for her services to children's literature. She has been described by *The Times* as 'a national treasure'. Malorie Blackman is the Children's Laureate 2013–15.

# Contents

# Spiders are... Beautiful

*Tap! Tap! Tap!* I didn't bother to turn round. *Tap! Tap! Tap!* There it was again. Someone was tapping on the shop window and whoever it was, they obviously weren't going to go away until they had my full attention. With a sigh, I turned round.

It was a boy. A boy who blinked a lot.

He wore round glasses and he had the most serious face I'd ever seen. The boy looked at me. I looked at him. He tapped again very gently on the shop window with his fingernail and smiled – a genuine,

friendly, admiring
smile. And that's
when I knew!
This boy was all
right! I beamed
back at him, giving
him my biggest, cheesiest, fangiest grin.

Come into the shop, I thought. *Please* come in and buy me.

I didn't want to build up my hopes. Lots of people – men and women, boys and girls – had tapped on the window and waved. Some even smiled. But none of them ever came into the shop to buy me. Mind you, a lot more people had banged on the window and looked at me with horror or disgust. But all those people who didn't like the way I looked obviously needed glasses. And if they already wore glasses, then they obviously needed *stronger* glasses. I am without a doubt the most gorgeous spider I know! I am probably the most drop-dead gorgeous spider in the world. What am I saying?! I'm *definitely* the most drop-dead gorgeous spider in the whole *universe*!

But I was also the most fed-up spider in the universe. I was tired of sitting in a tank in the pet shop window. I wanted to live somewhere else. Living in a tank in the pet shop was boring. And, worse than that, it was lonely. I had a long-distant memory of the sun and the sky in another place with hundreds of my family all around me. But now it was

just me. And the memory was so distant, I sometimes wondered if it was just a dream. How I longed to live somewhere where I'd see the sun and the sky during the day and the stars and the moon at night.

But it was no good wishing for something like that. If anyone did buy me, I'd be in a tank indoors and what I'd see above me would be a ceiling. Still, at least it'd be better than an empty fish tank in a pet shop.

The boy watching me mouthed, "*Wait there!*" – like I was going anywhere! He straightened up and practically ran into the shop.

Obviously my biggest, cheesiest, fangiest smile had worked!

"How much for the tarantula in the window?" the boy asked.

"Ten pounds," said Mrs Bucket, who owned the pet shop.

The boy's shoulders slumped. "I've only got five."

"I could give you two very attractive goldfish for that price," Mrs Bucket suggested.

The boy shook his head. "No, I wanted the tarantula."

"Why?" Mrs Bucket shook her head and wrinkled up her nose. "It's so hairy and ugly."

What a cheek!

"Are you kidding? Spiders are beautiful," said the boy. "And that tarantula is the most beautiful spider I've ever seen."

This boy obviously had very good taste – and eyes that worked perfectly!

Mrs Bucket scratched her head thoughtfully.

"Well, I've had a lot of offers for that spider . . ." – which was a lie! – '. . . but I can tell she'll have a good home with you, so she's yours for exactly five pounds."

"Really?" The boy started hopping up and down. "She's really mine? Oh, thank you." He started digging into his pockets and taking out all kinds of loose change. Soon the counter in front of Mrs Bucket was covered with coins. She didn't even bother to count them.

She swept the coins off the counter into her huge cupped hand and dumped the lot into the till.

"Help yourself," she said, pointing in my direction.

The boy ran over, lifted the lid off the fish tank and scooped me up.

"Do you know how to look after tarantulas?" Mrs Bucket asked.

"Yes, I do. I've read all about them."

And the boy ran out of the shop as if he was afraid that Mrs Bucket would change her mind about selling me off so cheaply.

"Hi, I'm Nathan," the boy said once he was safely away from the shop. "Let me see if I can guess your name."

"Hello. I'm Fangella," I told him.

He looked at me thoughtfully. "Legs?" he pondered.

"My name is Fangella," I repeated.

"Chewy?" Nathan wondered.

I sighed. Obviously, Nathan couldn't understand a word I was saying. I don't know why I was disappointed. I'd never yet met a human who could understand me when I spoke. Why should Nathan be any different?

"I've got it! I'll call you Fangella – or Fangs for short!"

I stared at Nathan. I could hardly believe it. Could this human understand me after all? Maybe not directly, but we had to be able to communicate on some level. How else could he have known my name? My name is much too uncommonly wonderful to guess. I could tell this was going to be the start of a beautiful friendship.

With me resting in one of his hands, Nathan glanced down at his watch. "Oh no! I'm late!" he groaned. Cupping his hands around me, he started running.

"You're going to love it at my house, Fangs," puffed Nathan. "You can sleep under my bed if you like. I'll keep you in a box with air-holes until I can get a proper home for you."

It sounded OK. It wasn't the stars
and the sun and the sky. But it
wasn't the pet shop either.

"There's just one
problem."

Nathan slowed
down a bit
– thank

goodness. "I'm not quite sure how I'm going to get you past my mum. But don't worry, I'll come up with something. It's just that . . . well, Mum's not too keen on spiders. When she finds them in the bath, they get washed straight down the plug hole and when she finds one on the carpet it goes CRU-UNN-CCHH under her foot."

And in that moment I knew that we were in TROUBLE.

# Spiders are ... Amazing

"Did you fall out of bed this morning and land on your head or something?" Nathan's mum asked.

Nathan and his family were having breakfast, not that Nathan was doing much eating. He turned to his dad for help. His dad took a quick sip of coffee and shook his head. "Don't look at me, Nathan. You're on your own with this one," he said.

Nathan sighed and turned to his mum to try again. "*Please*, Mum. *Please*," he begged.

"No! How many more times?" his mum said, exasperated. "Why can't you ask for a dog or a cat? At least that's a bit more normal."

"Would you let me have a dog or a cat?" Nathan asked.

"Nope! But at least I could understand you asking for one of those, instead of a …a …" Nathan's mum shivered. "Ugh! It makes my skin crawl just to think about it."

I wondered if I should crawl up onto the table from where I was hiding, I mean, from where I was *sitting* on Nathan's leg.

Maybe if his mum saw how beautiful and hairy I was, she'd change her mind.

"And what about Nadine?" Nathan's mum asked.

"What about her?" Nathan leaned across to see the baby sitting in her own special chair at his mum's side. I lifted two legs to wave to Nadine.

She cooed (at least that's what it sounded like!) and waved back. I like babies. And babies seem to like me too.

"You wouldn't like a great big spider crawling all over her face, would you?" said Nathan's mum.

"Nadine wouldn't mind," said Nathan.

"*I* would."

"But, Mum . . ."

"Why d'you want one anyway?" Nathan's other sister, Shelby, interrupted. "All they do is crawl and creep and wriggle about. They're not even interesting."

"Are you kidding? Spiders are amazing. They're tons more interesting than any dog or cat," said Nathan, enthusiastically. "D'you know how they eat? They inject their food — like insects and things — with a deadly venom to paralyse them and then they suck out all their juices whilst they're still alive. Isn't that great?"

I looked up at Nathan and shook my head. What a twit! Somehow I didn't think his mum would admire the way I ate my food — and I was right. A stunned silence filled the kitchen.

Nathan looked at the horrified faces of his mum and sister, and the resigned expression on his dad's face — and realized he'd messed up!

"Nathan, that's not the argument I would've used to try and persuade your mother." His dad shook his head. "That's a teensy bit more information than she needed."

"Mum, you're not going to let him have one, are you?" Shelby pleaded.

"Not in my lifetime, no," Nathan's mum replied.

"Well, I'd better go before I miss my train." Nathan's dad stood up and popped

his last piece of toast into his mouth. He kissed Nathan's mum, and came round the table to kiss Shelby, then Nathan, goodbye. But before he straightened up, he whispered, "Nathan, I'd get rid of that spider on your leg *fast* if I were you, before your mother sees it."

He straightened up and winked at Nathan. After a glance down at his watch, he ran out of the house, calling out, "Bye, everyone! See you all in a few hours."

The moment the front door was slammed shut, Nathan's mum turned to Nathan. "What did your dad just say?"

"Nothing."

"Nathan, you're not to bring a spider anywhere near this house. D'you understand?"

"But, Mum, spiders are really—" Nathan began to protest.

"I don't want to hear it! I want you to promise you won't buy a spider of any size, shape or description," Nathan's mum insisted.

"And he's not even talking about an ordinary spider at that. He wants to buy a great big, hairy *scary* tarantula," Shelby sniffed. "I don't think so!"

Me? Scary? I am big and hairy, yes, but scary? No way! I am magnificent. I am stunning. Every hair on my body is a joy to behold.

"Nathan, promise," his mum ordered.

I could see that Nathan was doing some fast thinking. "I promise not to go out and buy any spiders," Nathan said, carefully.

"Hmm . . ." Nathan's mum's eyes narrowed. "And that includes getting one of your friends to buy one for you. I know all your tricks, Nathan. Just make sure you keep your promise."

"I will."

Nathan nodded. He scooped me up and escaped upstairs.

"Fangs," he said, shaking his head. "We have some lightning-fast thinking to do."

# Spiders are . . . Useful

"Come on, Fangs, you've got to help me. What am I going to do? I don't want to take you back to the pet shop. I won't do it. But we have to do something to win Mum over."

I scuttled up the bed to sit on Nathan's pillow. Nathan lay down on his back, and let me crawl up his face to sit on his forehead.

"What we have to do is convince Mum of how much good you can do," Nathan decided.

"I could have this house cleared of all

creepy-crawlies in a couple of hours flat," I told him. "Why don't you tell your mum that?"

Nathan lay still, his face as long as rainy fortnight. Suddenly, without warning, he sat bolt upright, his eyes wide. I fell off his face and into his lap. It was lucky I didn't break one of my eight lovely legs!

"Watch what you're doing!" I said, crossly.

A slow smile crept over Nathan's face.

"Fangs, I'm a genius! It's so simple! Why didn't I think of it before?" Nathan scooped me up and carefully whirled me around the room until my head was spinning.

Placing me gently in his shirt pocket this time, Nathan tiptoed downstairs to the kitchen. Luckily, it was empty.

"The first thing I have to do is find a large container."

I wasn't sure whether Nathan was talking to me or himself. What did he have in mind? I must admit I couldn't help feeling just a little anxious. He opened all the cupboards but couldn't find anything that was suitable.

He opened the fridge.

"Eureka!" he beamed. "That's perfect!"

I didn't see what was so perfect about the strawberry jam jar he took out of the fridge. He spooned the tiny bit of jam left in the jar straight into his mouth.

Then he washed the jar out in some hot water and went out into the garden.

"Now for phase two," Nathan whispered. "This won't take long."

He obviously thought that phase two would only last a few minutes, but half an hour later he was *still* at it. I began to creep out of his shirt pocket.

"No, not yet." Nathan gently pushed me back down. "I'll tell you when it's safe to come out."

Nathan got back to the task at hand. By now, I'd figured out what he was up to. I tried to tell him it wasn't a very good idea but this time he really didn't hear me. I don't think he wanted to hear me. And the more he put into the jam jar, the more worried I became.

At long last the jam jar was full. Grinning, Nathan went back into the house. He listened out for sounds of his mum and sisters.

"It's OK," he whispered to me. "They're all upstairs. Fangs, this is it!"

He took out the jam jar, unscrewed the lid and tipped its contents over the kitchen floor. All the worms and caterpillars and maggots and beetles and ants and woodlice he'd collected scampered and scurried and scattered in every direction. Nathan grinned as he watched the wave of insects flood out to every corner of the kitchen.

I looked down at the floor. By now, I knew enough about humans — especially mums — to know that Nathan's mum wasn't going to be too thrilled when she saw the state of her kitchen. Still, if I was going to be booted out of the house or tipped down the toilet, I'd make sure I had a full stomach first! I usually liked my food to be a bit bigger but I reckoned that under the circumstances I couldn't be too choosy. I tried to climb down Nathan's chest towards all the delicious wriggling treats at his feet.

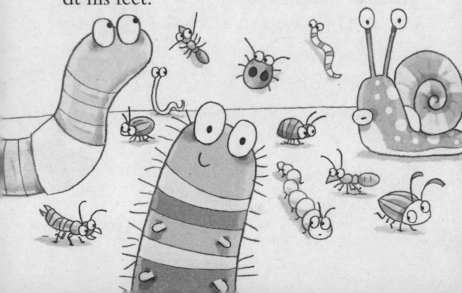

"Not yet, Fangs. Mum's got to see all these creepy-crawlies first."

Which was exactly what I was afraid of!

Mum's footsteps sounded from above.

She was coming downstairs, humming to herself.

"Come on, Fangs. Let's go back into the garden. We've got to pretend that all this is a real surprise." Avoiding the insects all over the floor, Nathan ran out into the garden, leaving the kitchen door open.

I couldn't help thinking that if Nathan's mum was in for a shock, then Nathan was

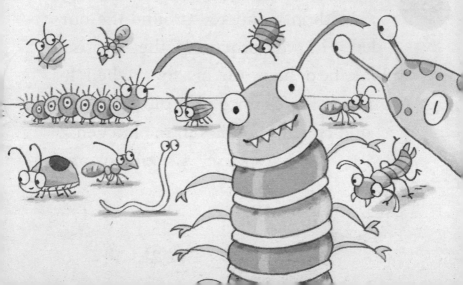

in for an even bigger one!

"I can see it all now. Mum'll walk into the kitchen, see all the creatures on the floor and wish that she'd let me have my spider. Then I'll produce you from my pocket and set you to work." Nathan grinned at me. "In no time at all you'll eat up all the insects in the kitchen. And then Mum'll see that spiders are *useful*. She'll probably give me a hug and call me a clever boy and all that other mum stuff!"

Nathan wandered around the garden. He was practising the surprised look he'd have on his face when his mum asked him about all the insects and creepy-crawlies in the kitchen.

"The suspense is killing me!

What's Mum doing?" said
Nathan. "Probably watching telly."

But we didn't have long to wait.

"ARRRGGGGHHHHH!"
Nathan's mum's shriek
could probably be
heard on the moon.
"NATHAN!
NATHAN, GET
IN HERE!"

"Watch this!" Nathan
said, excitely. "Now all
we have to do is act as if the insects
all over the kitchen floor are a big
surprise to us as well."

"NATHAN, COME HERE –
NOW."

Nathan grinned. "This is it, Fangs. This
is your chance to *shine*."

He forced the smile from his face.

He didn't want his mum to know that he knew anything about the state of the kitchen.

"NATHAN!"

Nathan walked into the house. He looked at his mum and I looked up at him from his pocket and in that instant I knew Nathan's plan wasn't going to work. I crawled slowly up the pocket and peeped out to see what was going on.

"Mum, what is it? What's the matter?" Shelby came running in, holding her baby sister, Nadine. Shelby took one look at the kitchen floor, shrieked like a screech owl, and dashed off again.

Nathan's mum's lips were turned in and her cheeks were puffed out and her eyes glared like lasers. The creepy-crawlies were all over the floor and climbing up the cupboard doors. And just when I thought it couldn't get any worse – it did! A caterpillar dropped down from the ceiling into Mum's hair.

"AAAAARRRRGGGGHHHHH!"

This time the scream could've been heard on Pluto.

And she went *crazy*. Absolutely nuts. She danced about, her hands sweeping over her head as she tried to knock the caterpillar out of her hair. Nathan started backing out of the kitchen. Somehow he knew that this was *not* the moment to produce and introduce me. The caterpillar fell out of Mum's hair. I'm sure it jumped rather than waiting to be pushed.

"Nathan, don't you dare take another step." Mum's voice sounded really strange. Kind of gurgly and gaspy. "Did you do this?" From the look on Mum's face she already knew the answer.

Nathan nodded slowly.

"You will get rid of every insect in this kitchen if it takes you the rest of your life!" Mum looked like a volcano on the verge of exploding. "And then you will scrub the work surfaces, the cupboard doors and the kitchen floor until they are spotless. Do you understand?"

Nathan nodded.

"DO YOU UNDERSTAND?"

"Yes, Mum."

Nathan nodded faster this time.

"I'm going upstairs . . ."

Mum lifted her foot so that the worm next to it couldn't crawl over her slipper.

"I am going upstairs to have a long shower and wash my hair. When I come back down, I want this kitchen the way I left it an hour ago."

Mum tiptoed out of the kitchen, doing her best to avoid each and every creepy-crawly. When she reached the hall she turned to Nathan, gave him a furious look, and slammed the door shut behind her.

# Spiders are . . . Necessary

"My fingers ache. My arms ache. My back aches," Nathan complained. "There's only a single hair at the top of my head which *doesn't* ache."

I'd eaten as many creatures as I could, but even I couldn't finish all of them.

"Never mind your aches and pains," I told him. "What're we going to do?"

Nathan sighed. "After all these insects in the kitchen, Mum probably hates the idea of having a spider in the house even more now."

"I'm not an insect," I said, indignantly.

"For one thing, insects have six legs and I have eight."

"I know you're an arachnid, not an insect," Nathan continued, "but as far as Mum's concerned, you creep-crawl about which makes you a creepy-crawly."

Nathan finally got rid of the rest of the insects and trudged upstairs to his bedroom. His mum had already had three showers and we could hear the shower in the bathroom starting up again.

"Come on, Nathan. Think!" I told him.

"Come on, Nathan. Think!" Nathan told himself.

And we both sat there on Nathan's bed, desperately trying to come up with another plan. Time passed and neither of us had come up with a single thing. The handle on the bedroom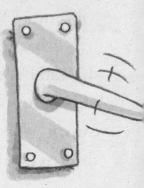

door turned. Nathan only just had time
to hide me between the headboard and
the pillow before his mum came into the
room. She stood there, rubbing her wet
hair with a towel.

"Shelby, Nadine and I are going to the park," she said. "If you promise to behave yourself you can come with us."

"I promise," Nathan said at once.

"We'll set off in about half an hour," said Nathan's mum. "See if you can keep out of trouble until then."

And with that she left the room.

"What I need to do is persuade Mum that she can't do without you," Nathan said slowly.

"You tried that, remember?" I told him.

"Let me have another crack at her." Nathan leaped off his bed. "I'll take you out as far as the landing so that you can listen, but you've got to stay upstairs and out of sight."

Nathan took me out to the landing and left me at the top of the stairs. He ran down to the living room. No way was I going to stay put. I should be down there, in the thick of things, I decided. So I made my way downstairs.

"Mum, please can I have a tarantula?" Nathan asked.

I sighed. Couldn't he be a bit more subtle about it?

"Nathan, after what you just did I wouldn't even let you have a toy spider. I wouldn't even let you have a *drawing* of a spider," his mum fumed.

"Oh please, Mum. I promise you wouldn't even see it. I'd keep it in my bedroom in a proper cage."

"I do go in there occasionally to tidy the place," Mum sniffed.

"I'd keep it under the bed until I got home from school," Nathan persisted.

"Nathan, you must be nuts! There is no way in the world I'm going to let you keep a giant spider in this house," his mum replied.

"But Mum, tarantulas aren't like ordinary spiders . . ." Nathan began.

"No, they're bigger!" said Shelby.

Nathan's mum raised her eyebrows. "They have eight legs and they spin webs and they creep and crawl about, don't they?"

"Tarantulas don't use webs to catch bugs for their dinner! They hunt their food and spin lovely silk nests as their homes, that's all," said Nathan.

I walked to the doorway and looked in.

"So how do they catch their food?" Shelby asked.

Nathan glared at his sister. I could see he was irritated. He was trying to persuade his mum to let him get a tarantula. He didn't want Shelby putting in her two pence worth.

"If you must know, they hunt for their food. They lie in wait in burrows or go out searching for small mammals and insects and birds," Nathan explained.

"Aren't tarantulas poisonous?" Shelby asked, suspiciously.

"They're venomous, not poisonous, but their venom doesn't kill humans," Nathan said.

"Venomous!" Mum exclaimed. "What if it bit Nadine?"

"Spiders very rarely bite people. Besides, Mum, spiders are necessary. Insects would take over the world if it wasn't for spiders.

Think of all the insects in the house they eat up. You hate flies and woodlice and stuff in the house," Nathan tried.

"I also hate spiders in the house. Remember?" Mum said. "Wait a minute! Is that the reason I had all those creepy, nasty, ugly things in my kitchen?"

Nathan didn't answer. I wondered if maybe now was a good time to beat a hasty retreat. I looked around. Nadine sat in her stroller by the front door, busy counting her toes.

"So that's what all that nonsense was about!" Mum said, crossly. "Was I meant to scream for a spider to get rid of all those creepy-crawlies and then you'd rush straight out to the pet shop and buy one?"

It was definitely time to leave.

"Or did you have a spider closer to hand?" Nathan's mum asked softly.

Nathan nodded slowly.

"Where is it, Nathan?" his mum asked.

"She's upstairs on the landing," Nathan admitted.

'And what kind of spider are we talking about?" asked his mum.

"A . . . tarantula. Called Fangs."

'AARRGGGHHH!" Shelby jumped up and stood on the sofa, hopping from foot to foot.

Nadine and I looked at each other and shook our heads. What a big fuss about nothing! But now that Shelby and her mum knew about me, they wouldn't rest until I was out of the house by the most painful route possible.

"Nathan, go and get that spider *now*," his mum ordered. "And I'll be right behind you to make sure that you do."

"I'm not moving from this sofa until that spider is out of the house," screamed

Shelby. Anyone would think I ate *people* from the way she was carrying on.

Nathan and his mum came out of the living room. I had to get out of that house before Nathan's mum found me. But how? *How?*

# Spiders are . . . Brave

Nadine held me in her hands and stroked my back, but she didn't have my full attention. I watched Nathan run upstairs, followed a few stairs behind by his mum. He came to an abrupt stop when he got to the landing.

"She's gone!"

"What d'you mean 'she's gone!'?"

"I left Fangs right here." Nathan pointed to the top of the stairs. "And I told her not to move. But don't worry, Mum, she's very tame and friendly and she wouldn't hurt anyone."

"I am going to the park with Shelby and Nadine." Nathan's mum's voice was as hard as flint. "When I get back I want to see your . . . spider in a jar with the lid firmly screwed on so that I can get rid of it myself."

"But, Mum . . ."

"No buts." Nathan's mum waved aside his objection. "Catch that spider and have it ready for me to get rid of. You are in serious trouble already, Nathan. Don't make it worse. *I want that spider.*"

Nathan's mum marched downstairs and grabbed her jacket off a coat peg by the door. I crawled out of Nadine's hand and moved deeper down into her stroller until Nadine was practically sitting on me. But I reckoned being sat on was better than being found by her mum.

"Shelby, come on. We're going out," Nathan's mum called.

Shelby came running out of the living room like a ballet dancer on tiptoes. She grabbed her jacket and was out of the front door before you could say 'I hate spiders!' Nathan's mum wheeled the stroller out of the house, saying to Nathan, "Find that spider!"

Nathan's mum pushed Nadine and me down the garden path with Shelby in front of us. I was still wondering how on earth I was going to escape without Nathan's mum spotting me and jumping up and down on me, when all of a sudden I heard the sound of angry yelping.

I risked crawling out from behind Nadine to peep out of the stroller – and what I saw made my blood run icy cold.

A pit-bull terrier was charging towards us and it was in a real rage. I saw why at once. Flying just behind the enraged dog was a wasp. The pit-bull and the wasp had got into a fight and, from the look of it, the wasp was winning. From the mad look on the pit-bull's face, he'd been stung, and now he was heading straight for us . . .

Shelby screamed and hid behind her mum. Her mum tried to move Nadine's stroller out of the way but it was as if all her fingers had suddenly become thumbs and the stroller had taken on a life of its own and refused to move. The pit-bull terrier was still charging in our direction. I crawled up Nadine's shoulder. Nadine was bawling. She could see the dog coming and she was terrified. I couldn't blame her. That pit-bull was howling mad and wanted to lash out. It wanted to sink its teeth into the first thing in its path which, unfortunately, was Nadine. It came closer and closer, baring its teeth. Nadine's mum tried to get in front of the stroller but her cardigan got caught up in one of the handles. I could feel her trying to swing the stroller around, but she couldn't. Meanwhile, the pit-bull had only one thing on its mind – biting Nadine. I scampered on top of Nadine's head. The pit-bull was only half a metre away. I thought I heard Nathan's voice but I had to concentrate on the pit-bull. No way was that dog going to get to Nadine. I had to time this exactly right.

The pit-bull opened

its mouth wider. I jumped onto its face
and ran up to the top of his head. The pit-
bull obviously agreed with Nathan's mum
when it came to big spiders. Terrified,
it veered to the left and crashed into
Nathan's mum's garden wall.

The dog collapsed in a dazed heap as his head hit the bricks, and I scurried over to the stroller. Nadine scooped me up and hugged me to her. I could hardly breathe, but I didn't mind.

"Nadine, let it go. Give it to Mummy." Nathan's mum tried to take me out of her hands but Nadine started howling.

By this time we were surrounded by people, and a man from the next-door house ran out saying, "It's OK. I've called the police and the RSPCA."

Nathan came running over as well. It was total chaos!

"Nathan, is that your tarantula? Get rid of it – NOW!" Nathan's mum screamed at him. "It's going to harm Nadine."

"No, she isn't," Nathan protested. "In fact, Fangs just saved Nadine from that dog. I saw it all from my bedroom window."

"That's true, Mum." To my surprise, even Shelby was on my side. "If it wasn't for Fangs . . ."

"Fans! Fans!" said Nadine, hugging me tighter.

By this time an RSPCA van had pulled up next to us and the man and woman who came out were busy muzzling the dog, who was still in a daze.

"Mum, please let Fangella stay. She wouldn't hurt a fly," Nathan pleaded.

His mum raised her eyebrows.

"Well, maybe a fly," Nathan admitted. "But she wouldn't hurt any of us. Please can we keep her. *Please?*"

"Shelby?" Nathan's mum asked.

Shelby frowned. She looked from me to Nathan and back again. "I don't want it in my bedroom or anywhere where I could trip over it."

"Neither do I," said Nathan's mum. "All right, Nathan. You can keep your spider – but only on one condition."

"Yes, Mum!" Nathan said at once.

"Hold on. You haven't heard the condition yet." Nathan's mum smiled. "Your spider has to live at the bottom of the garden. You can build a place for it to feed and sleep and it can run around the garden when I'm not there! Is it a deal?"

"Yes, Mum," Nathan said, beaming.

And he wasn't the only one who was grinning. I was going to stay *outside*. I'd see the stars and the sky and the moon and the sun again. Yippee! Nathan managed to prise me away from his sister's grasp, and I gave him one of my cheesy, fangy grins.

"Well done, Fangs!" he said. "See, Mum! Not only are spiders beautiful, amazing, useful and necessary, but Fangs is the bravest spider of them all!"

And I wasn't about to argue!

**Fang-tastic Spider Facts!**

• **Fangs** is a tarantula; tarantulas are particularly big and hairy arachnids (spiders) which are found in the wild in the United States, South and Central America, throughout Africa, Asia and all over Australia. Some species of tarantula are found in parts of southern Europe too.

• The biggest known spider in the world is the goliath birdeater: a kind of tarantula with a leg span (from the end of the front right leg to the end of the back left leg) of up to 28 centimetres and which can weigh over 170 grams, about as much as a Frisbee! Despite their name, goliath birdeaters mainly eat earthworms.

• There are over 800 known species of tarantula – the most recently discovered was a giant tarantula found in Sri Lanka in 2013.

• Tarantulas can look a bit scary with their large bodies and long, hairy legs, but most tarantula are harmless to humans – the venom in their fangs is weaker than the venom in a bee sting.

• When tarantulas are threatened, to defend themselves they can flick urticating bristles – hairs which cause irritation – at the face of a predator.

• As they grow, tarantulas moult – they shed their hardened outer layer which gives their body strength and shape. It is in this way that they can replace their urticating bristles and even any legs they may have lost!

• Unlike smaller spiders, tarantulas don't use webs as traps, but instead hunt and ambush their prey.

• Tarantulas mainly eat insects but the biggest tarantulas hunt other animals like lizards, mice, birds and even small snakes!

• Although tarantulas don't make webs in the same way that house spiders do, they do spin silk which they use to line their burrows and protect their eggs.

• As is true for many creatures, several species of tarantula are endangered because human activities like cutting down forests have led to the loss of their natural habitat. We must work hard to protect the environment to make sure that these amazing creatures can continue to flourish in the wild.